Book 2

All-Star Cheerleaders

Save the Best for Last, Abby

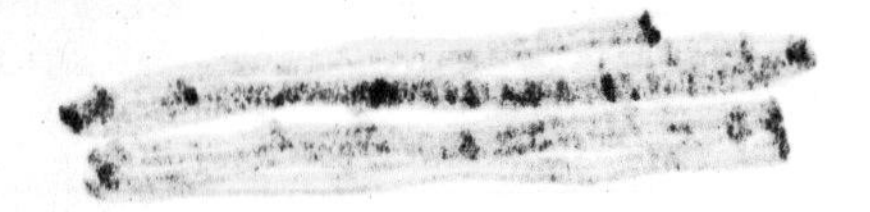

All-Star Cheerleaders

Book #1 Tick Tock, Taylor!

Book #2 Save the Best for Last, Abby

Book #3 Just So, Brianna

Do your best and forget the rest!

For Maureen

Kane Miller, A Division of EDC Publishing

For information contact:
Kane Miller, A Division of EDC Publishing
PO Box 470663
Tulsa, OK 74147-0663
www.kanemiller.com
www.edcpub.com
www.usbornebooksandmore.com

Library of Congress Control Number: 2011932585

Printed in the United States of America

1 2 3 4 5 6 7 8 9 10

ISBN: 978-1-61067-001-2

Book 2

All-Star Cheerleaders

Save the Best for Last, Abby

Written by Anastasia Suen
Illustrated by Hazel Mitchell

Kane Miller
A DIVISION OF EDC PUBLISHING

SOPHIA
LIV
EMMA
KAYLA
MADDIE
BIG D ELITE
ABBY
TAYLOR
BRIANNA

CHAPTER 1
Thursday Practice

Abby and her little sister Emma sat on the back seat of the car. They were going to the Big D Elite Gym for cheerleading practice. Mom drove them there after school twice a week.

Abby pulled her long red hair back into a ponytail and fastened it with a rubber band. Coach Tammy insisted they keep their hair up when they cheered.

"Mom," said Abby, "can Taylor sleep over

this weekend?" Abby and Taylor were best friends. They had been cheering together since they were three.

"That's fine with me," said Mom. "I'll talk to Taylor's mom at the gym."

"Can I have a friend over too?" asked Emma.

"You know the rule," said Mom, "only one friend over at a time."

"Why does Abby get to have her friend sleep over?" said Emma.

"She asked first," said Mom.

"Abby is always first," said Emma. She crossed her arms and stuck out her lower lip.

"I'm the oldest," said Abby. Abby was eight, and Emma was only six. "I can't help it if I was born first."

"It's not fair," said Emma.

"Now, girls," said Mom, and she sighed. "We've been over this a thousand times.

Someone had to be born first, but we love you both the same. We *do*." She drove into the parking lot.

"But first is better," said Emma.

"First is fabulous," said Mom. "We're very proud of Abby."

Abby smiled.

"But what about me?" asked Emma.

Mom turned off the car. "Now, Emma," said Mom. "What do I always say?"

Emma shrugged.

"We saved the best for last," said Mom. "We love you both! Now let's go in for practice. "

Abby looked at Emma. *Will that make her stop?*

Emma looked at Mom. Then she looked at Abby. "OK, OK," said Emma. She opened the car door. "Can I have a sleepover next weekend?"

"Of course," said Mom.

"But, Mom," said Abby. "Then Taylor can't come over that weekend. She always comes over after the competition."

"Emma asked first," said Mom. "You know we take turns in this family."

"Yes, I know," said Abby, as she walked across the parking lot. They all went into the gym together. Mom headed for the chairs at the side of the room. The mothers always sat there and chatted during practice.

Abby and Emma walked across the big blue mat to put down their gym bags. *It's not fair,* thought Abby. *Why can't Taylor come over next weekend too? She always comes over after competitions. Emma only asked because I asked first.* Abby looked over at her sister. Emma's ponytail was coming undone.

"Let me fix your hair," said Abby.

Emma put her arm up. "No! I'll do it myself."

Emma put down her bag. She reached up, took out her rubber band, then redid her ponytail.

"It's crooked," said Abby. "Let me ..."

"No!" said Emma. "Leave me alone!" She ran to the side of the mat.

"Hey, Abby," said Taylor.

"Taylor," said Abby. "My mom said yes! You can sleep over this weekend!"

"Yay," said Taylor. The girls looked at their moms and waved. Their moms waved back.

"What's up with Emma?" asked Taylor.

"Why did she run away from you?"

Abby shook her head. "She's mad because I get to have a sleepover first."

"I hope she doesn't stay mad," said Taylor.

Abby sighed. "I hope not."

Clap, clap, clap!

Coach Tammy clapped her hands. "Let's start practice."

Abby and the girls on the Glitter squad ran to their places on the mat. They did their warm-up stretches. Coach Tammy said you should always warm up your muscles before you used them. It helped prevent injury.

"Now that we're warmed up," said Coach Tammy, "let's do our routine."

The girls ran over to the edge of the mat and lined up.

"Now do it right," said Sophia. She always stood behind Abby and Taylor in the line.

Abby looked at Taylor. Taylor rolled her eyes. Sophia was eight, just like they were, but she was so bossy!

"OK," said Coach Tammy. "Now walk out onto the mat two by two."

Abby watched as Emma and Brianna led the squad onto the mat. *You're first now, Emma.*

The bases followed the two flyers. Kayla and Liv were next. Then Abby and Taylor walked onto the mat. Sophia and

Maddie were last.

Abby walked over to her place. She put her head down and waited for the music to start.

Coach Tammy turned on the music. Sound filled the gym. After a few notes, a deep voice said, “Presenting … Big D Elite Glitter!”

That was their cue! Everyone started moving.

Two and a half minutes later, they were done. That was the time limit for each routine. They had to impress the judges and make all of their points in just two and a half minutes.

Coach Tammy clapped her hands. “That looked great,” she said. “Now we’re going to learn a new dance routine.”

Why? thought Abby. *We won first place last month with this one. That didn’t happen last year. Why are we changing it?*

CHAPTER 2

Something Fancy

"Gather round," said Coach Tammy.

The Glitter girls came over and sat in the center of the mat.

"You did so well at the last competition," said Coach Tammy, "I'm going to make the last sequence a bit fancier."

"We need it," said Sophia.

No, we don't, thought Abby.

"Go to your places for the last sequence," said Coach Tammy.

BIG
D
ELITE
BIG
D
ELITE

"We're ready to win," said Sophia.

What does she mean? thought Abby. *We won last time.*

"See how you're all facing the judges?" said Coach Tammy.

Yes, we are, thought Abby. *We want them to see how good we are.*

"Let's make a circle instead," said Coach Tammy. "I'll walk around and place you."

Coach Tammy walked over to the girls in the front row. She moved Emma and Brianna forward on the mat. She turned them at an angle so they each looked at a different corner of the gym.

Then she walked over and turned Kayla to face one wall. She moved Maddie to face the other.

"Oh, I get it," said Abby.

"It's just like our other circle," said Taylor.

"When we do the cartwheels," said Abby.

"No cartwheels now," said Coach Tammy. Then she moved Abby over and turned her to face the opposite corner.

Coach Tammy placed Taylor, Liv and Sophia.

Abby looked over her shoulder at the squad. Everyone was facing a different direction!

"Turn around now, Abby," said Coach Tammy.

"OK," said Abby. She turned back.

"Now we're ready," said Coach Tammy. She started counting. "Five, six, seven, eight."

Abby and the girls started to move.

One, two, three, four, arms up.

Five, six, seven, eight, arms out.

Coach Tammy clapped her hands. "That looks great!" She put her hands on her hips. "Now let's change it just a bit."

Abby looked over Taylor. *Again?*

"Turn around to face the center," said Coach Tammy.

All of the Glitter girls turned around.

"Now take two steps in," said Coach Tammy.

The girls moved closer to the center.

"Great," said Coach Tammy. "Now this time, turn on four."

"Which way?" asked Abby.

"To your right," said Coach Tammy. "Watch me."

Coach Tammy counted down. "Five, six, seven, eight." Then she did the moves. "One, two, three, arms out." As Coach Tammy put her arms out, she turned to the right and faced the wall.

I can do that, thought Abby.

Coach Tammy did the last four moves facing the wall.

"OK, girls, let's give it a try," said Coach Tammy. "Here we go. Five, six, seven, eight."

The Glitter girls began to move.

One, two, three, four, arms up and turn.

Five, six, seven, eight and arms out.

Coach Tammy clapped her hands. "That was wonderful!"

Abby and the girls turned to look at Coach Tammy.

"Now for the next thing," said Coach Tammy.

The next thing? Abby looked at Taylor. *What now?*

Taylor shook her head. *Who knows?*

"I want you to take a step as you turn," said Coach Tammy. "That will make the circle bigger. Can you do that?"

"Easy peasy," said Sophia.

Abby smiled at Taylor. *That* is *easy.* Taylor smiled back.

"Good," said Coach Tammy. "Let's do it now. Turn back to the center."

The Glitter girls all turned to face the center.

I'm ready, thought Abby.

"And here we go," said Coach Tammy. "Five, six, seven, eight."

They began to move.

One, two, three, four and turn and step. Arms up. Five, six, seven, eight and arms out.

Coach Tammy clapped her hands. "That looks marvelous!"

Then Abby heard a thumping sound.

"Oh, dear," said Coach Tammy.

Abby turned around. Emma had fallen over on the mat!

CHAPTER 3
What's Wrong with Emma?

Abby ran over to Emma. She was lying on the mat with her eyes closed. Her face was red. *What's wrong?*

"Emma," said Coach Tammy. She was kneeling on the mat next to Emma.

Emma didn't say anything.

"Go get your mom, Abby," said Coach Tammy.

Abby ran over to the chairs where the mothers were talking. "Mom, something's

BIG
BIG
D
ELITE

wrong with Emma!"

"Emma!" Mom stood up and ran across the mat. Abby followed her.

Mom knelt down next to Emma. "What happened, baby?" she said softly.

"Mom," said Emma. She opened her eyes.

"My poor baby," said Mom. She put her hand on Emma's forehead. "You're burning up with fever."

Fever, thought Abby. *How did she get that?*

"It looks like she caught that bug," said Coach Tammy.

"A bug?" said Emma.

"You're sick," said Mom.

Emma closed her eyes. "I don't feel so good."

"I had two tinies go home with fever today," said Coach Tammy. "It's going around."

Mom looked at Abby. "Get Emma's things, Abby. We're going home."

"Now?" said Abby. "It's the middle of practice."

"Now," said Mom. "Your sister has to come first."

"We'll still be here next week," said Coach Tammy. "We'll see you at practice then."

Abby walked over and picked up Emma's backpack. She put it over one shoulder. Then she picked up her own backpack and put it over the other shoulder. Abby looked at the Glitter girls gathered around Emma and Mom. Taylor was talking to Emma.

Taylor! Oh, no! What about the sleepover? Will Mom let Taylor sleep over if Emma is sick?

Abby quickly walked back to the middle of the mat. Coach Tammy and Mom were helping Emma stand up.

"Can Taylor still come over?" asked Abby.

"Not now, Abby," said Mom sharply. "Can't you see your sister is sick?"

Great, just great. Emma's sick, and Taylor can't come over. It's going to be a long weekend.

Tuesday Practice

"That was the longest weekend ever," said Abby. "Emma was sick the whole time. She was miserable."

"That's what you said on the phone," said Taylor. "But she looks better now."

"Finally," said Abby.

"When will we have our sleepover?" asked Taylor.

"Mom said I get next week, and Emma gets the week after that," replied Abby.

"So I come over after the competition?" said Taylor.

"Yes, it will be so fun!" said Abby.

"You better!" said a voice.

What was that? Abby looked across the mat. Sophia was wagging her finger at Kayla. "There she goes again."

"You know Sophia," said Taylor.

"Bossy," said Abby.

Taylor rolled her eyes.

Clap, clap, clap!

Coach Tammy clapped her hands. It was time for practice to start. "Let's warm up," said Coach Tammy.

The Glitter girls went to their places on the mat and stretched.

After they warmed up, it was time to do their routine again.

"The competition is this Saturday," said Coach Tammy. "Let's do our very best."

"Easy peasy," said Sophia.

Yes, we were number one last time, thought Abby.

All the girls walked over to the edge of the mat and lined up.

"Now, onto the mat," said Coach Tammy. "Make sure you smile for the judges."

Emma and Brianna led the way onto the mat. Abby smiled as she walked out to her place. Then she put her head down and waited for the music.

Here it comes.

"Presenting ... Big D Elite," said the deep voice.

Abby lifted her head and smiled at where the judges would be sitting. When it was her turn, she did the back limber. Then she helped Sophia and Kayla lift Emma into the air for the first stunt.

So far, so good.

As the music played, the squad did cartwheels, jumps and stunts.

We're going to be in first place again, thought Abby.

It was time for the cheer.

"Big D Elite, can't be beat.

We're the ones you want to meet!"

That's right, thought Abby. She walked to the side of the mat for the next stunt. Emma followed her.

But Sophia and Kayla were on the other side of the mat. *What's going on?*

BIG D ELITE
BIG D

COACH
BIG D ELITE
BIG D ELITE
BIG D ELITE

Coach Tammy turned off the music. Everyone turned to look at Abby and Emma.

"What are you doing over there?" said Sophia.

"Getting ready for the next stunt," said Abby.

"Don't you know anything?" asked Sophia. "We're doing the circle first and then the stunts."

"We are?" said Abby. She looked over at Coach Tammy.

"Let me do the coaching, Sophia," said Coach Tammy. She walked over to Abby and Emma. "We practiced it last week. Remember?"

"No, we didn't," said Emma. Tears came to her eyes.

Abby looked at her sister. *Oh, no, not again. You've been crying all weekend.*

Abby looked at Coach Tammy. "Emma was sick," said Abby. "We had to go home early."

"Oh, I'm so sorry," said Coach Tammy. "Of course." She leaned down and put her arm around Emma. "Are you feeling better now, Emma?"

Emma sniffed and looked up at Coach Tammy. "A little."

"That's good," said Coach Tammy. "We want you to be with us on Saturday."

"You do?" said Emma.

"Yes, we do," said Coach Tammy. "You're a great flyer."

"I am?" said Emma. She looked up at Coach Tammy.

Coach Tammy smiled. "Yes, you are."

What about me? Why does Emma get all the attention … again? Mom was at her side all weekend. And now Coach Tammy is telling Emma how great she is. Just because she cried.

Coach Tammy stood up. "OK, girls, let's show Emma and Abby how we do the last two parts."

"It's not hard," said Taylor.

"No, it's not," said Coach Tammy. "We just moved the stunts to the end. So the second circle comes after the cheer."

"Oh," said Abby. "That's not hard at all. I can do that."

Sophia walked up behind Abby. "You'd

better," said Sophia.

Abby frowned. *Can't she say anything nice?*

"Places, girls," said Coach Tammy. "Let's start with our cheer."

The Glitter girls stood in their places for the cheer. Then Coach Tammy counted. "Five, six, seven, eight."

"Big D Elite, can't be beat," they cheered as they moved. "We're the ones you want to meet!"

And now the circle, thought Abby. *Where do I go?* She looked at Taylor. *Oh, I remember.* Abby ran over and turned to face the wall.

Clap, clap, clap!

What's wrong? Abby turned to look at Coach Tammy.

Emma was standing off to the side, looking bewildered.

Coach Tammy walked over and took

Emma by the hand. "Over here, Emma," she said.

"What are we doing?" asked Emma. "I don't remember this."

"You're going to make us lose," said Sophia loudly.

"Now, Sophia," said Coach Tammy. She looked at the rest of the squad standing in front of her on the mat. "What do I always say?"

"Do your best and forget the rest," they replied.

"That's right," said Coach Tammy. "Let's do it one more time. Go back to your places for the cheer."

Everyone moved to their places. Abby looked over at Emma. *I hope she can do this. The competition is this Saturday.*

"Five, six, seven, eight," said Coach Tammy.

They did the cheer. Now it was time for

the new circle move.

Abby ran to her new spot. Then she turned and looked at Emma.

No! Emma's going the wrong way.

Abby ran over and took Emma's hand. She moved Emma to the right place. Then she ran back across the circle to her spot.

The other girls were already turning. *I have to catch up!*

Abby put her arms out and turned. She looked over at Taylor. *What are they doing? They added a step too?*

Abby took a step forward too. *Six, seven, eight and arms out.*

Now what? Abby looked at Sophia.

"The stunt," commanded Sophia. "Do the last stunt!"

Oh! Abby ran across the mat with Sophia. Kayla came over too. *But where's Emma?* Abby looked at the edge of the mat. Her sister looked back at her. Abby waved her hand. *Come on! It's time for the last stunt.*

Emma ran over. Abby, Kayla and Sophia lifted Emma into the air. Emma lifted her arms up.

"Now hold that pose for eight counts," said Coach Tammy.

Abby waited.

"OK," said Coach Tammy. "That looks good. Bases, bring your flyers back down."

Abby, Kayla and Sophia lowered Emma to the mat.

"What a disaster," said Sophia.

CHAPTER 6

Competition Saturday

"There they are," said Abby, as they walked through the arena doors.

"I see them," said Mom. She waved at Coach Tammy. "You two go on. I'll go inside and find a seat with the other parents." Mom kissed Abby and Emma on the forehead.

"Thanks, Mom," said Abby. Then she took Emma's hand and walked through the crowd.

"Well, it's about time," said Sophia. "Where were you two on Thursday?"

"Sick," said Abby. "I got what Emma had."

"But now you're better," said Taylor. She smiled.

"We'll see about that," said Sophia. She pointed her finger at Abby. "You know you have to practice if you want to be the best." Then she stormed off.

"Sophia is so mean," said Abby.

"I know," said Taylor. "She never has anything nice to say." Taylor gave Abby a hug. "I'm so glad you're here. I missed seeing you."

"I missed seeing you too. Talking on the phone isn't the same," said Abby.

"And what about the sleepover?" asked Taylor.

"If *you* don't get sick now, then you can still come over," said Abby.

"Yay!" said Taylor. She did a little jump in the air.

"Sleepover?" said Emma. She crossed her arms. "Why do you get to have the sleepover this weekend? It was supposed to be my turn."

Not that again, thought Abby. *How can I cheer her up so she doesn't start crying? I know. She loves it when everyone looks at her.*

Abby put her hands on Emma's shoulders. "But you get to be the flyer," said Abby. "Everyone looks at the flyer." Abby looked at Taylor. *Help me with this.*

"That's true," said Taylor. "Everyone looks at the flyer. You're on top!"

"Well," said Emma.

BIG D ELITE
BIG D ELITE
BIG D ELITE

"Abby," said Coach Tammy. "Time for your makeup."

"Coming," said Abby. She went over and sat in front of Coach Tammy.

"Close your eyes," said Coach Tammy.

"OK," said Abby.

Coach Tammy put silver-and-gold glitter eye shadow on Abby.

"Now pucker up," said Coach Tammy.

Abby opened her eyes. Then she puckered her lips. Coach Tammy put bright-red lipstick on Abby.

"Time for your star," said Coach Tammy. She put a glittery star on Abby's cheek.

"You look gorgeous," said Coach Tammy. Then she gave Abby a hug. "Send your sister over now. You two are the last ones to arrive."

Abby stood up and walked over to Emma. "Your turn, Emma," said Abby.

"Finally," said Emma. She looked around

at the other Glitter girls. "Everyone else is done. I'm last again."

Abby watched as her sister walked over to Coach Tammy. *I hope you don't make our squad come in last too.*

Warming Up

Clap, clap, clap!

Coach Tammy clapped her hands. "Let's line up," said Coach Tammy. "It's almost time for our warm-up."

Abby reached out and took Emma's hand. *I don't want you next to Sophia right now. We don't want any more crying.*

Then Abby reached out and grabbed Taylor's hand. *Here we go!*

The Glitter girls cheered as they walked

down the hallway of the arena.

"Big D Elite, can't be beat.

We're the ones you want to meet!"

Coach Tammy led the girls onto the arena floor.

A long black curtain hung from the ceiling. On one side of the curtain were the judges and the audience. On the other side was the practice area. The cheerleading squads there were warming up.

Abby watched as the other squads warmed up. The other minis were their competition.

"They look pretty good," said Taylor.

"Much better than last time," said Abby. She looked over at Sophia.

"Don't worry about Sophia," said Taylor. "You know how she is."

Abby sighed. "I know."

"It's our turn to warm up," said Coach Tammy.

Abby walked over to the mat and lined up with Taylor. Sophia and Kayla stood behind them.

"I hope you're not still sick," said Sophia. "I really want to win this."

Abby turned around. "I'm not sick anymore."

"You better not be," said Sophia. "It will be all your fault if we lose."

"What?" said Abby.

"Abby!" said Coach Tammy. "Let's go!" Abby turned around. The squad was walking onto the mat without her.

"Coming," said Abby. She followed the rest of the girls onto the mat.

"Make sure you smile at the judges as you walk onto the mat," said Coach Tammy.

Abby nodded her head. She knew what to do. She smiled as she walked onto the mat and found her place. Then she placed her hand on her hip and put her head down.

Coach Tammy turned on the music.

"Presenting ... Big D Elite," said the deep voice.

That was their cue. Abby lifted her head and started moving.

The Glitter girls did their back limbers. Then they did their first stunts. Abby lifted Emma high into the air. *You're the flyer, Emma. Everyone will be looking at you.*

After the stunts, Abby did her cartwheels. Then it was time for the four jumps, one in each direction. Then, more cartwheels. This time the girls did them in a circle. *I love this part*, thought Abby.

At the edge of the mat, she stood up. Then she turned and did three round offs in a row.

Time for the next stunt! Abby did a thigh stand and lifted Emma. *Up you go, little flyer!* Abby held onto her little sister as Emma lifted her leg out into the air. *And back down again.*

Then Kayla and Sophia came over. All three girls lifted Emma and carried her across the mat. They stopped when they reached the girls holding up Brianna. She was the other flyer.

Emma reached out and touched Brianna's hand. Abby and the other bases held on as Emma and Brianna did two more flyer moves. Then both of the flyers came back down to the mat.

Here comes the cheer.

"Big D Elite, can't be beat.

We're the ones you want to meet!"

One more stunt, and we're done. Abby walked over with Emma and …

Wait a minute, where is everyone?

CHAPTER 8

Mistakes

Coach Tammy clapped her hands. Then she turned off the music. "Abby and Emma," said Coach Tammy, "we moved the last stunts to the end. Remember?"

"Oh, yes, of course," said Abby.

Abby turned and looked at Emma. *Oh, no, don't start*

crying now. Everyone is looking at us.

"Let's do it again," said Coach Tammy. "Go back to the cheer. Then we'll finish."

"Come on, Emma," said Abby.

"But ..." Emma's voice was shaky.

Abby put her arm around Emma. "You can do this."

"Um, OK," said Emma.

Abby and Emma walked back to their places for the cheer.

"Five, six, seven, eight," said Coach Tammy.

Abby began to move.

"Big D Elite, can't be beat.

We're the ones you want to meet!"

And now ... Abby paused. *Oh, right. Now we do the old ending.*

Abby looked around the mat. *Where's Emma?*

Oh, no, she's moved over for the last stunt.

Abby quickly ran over to her sister "Emma!"

Emma looked up at Abby. Her eyes opened wide.

"Over here," said Abby. She grabbed Emma's hand.

Emma followed Abby over to a new spot on the mat. Then Abby let go of Emma's hand and ran back to her own spot in the circle.

"Abby," muttered Sophia.

"Keep going," said Coach Tammy.

Abby started moving. *One, two, three, four, arms out.*

"Turn," ordered Sophia.

What? Abby looked over at Sophia. She was facing the other direction.

Abby quickly turned.

"Take a step forward," commanded Sophia.

Abby took a step and tried to catch up. *Seven, eight and arms out.*

We're done! At last! Abby held the pose.

"Abby!" hissed Sophia.

Abby turned and looked. No one was standing near her. *Where did they go?* She turned around.

Kayla and Emma were standing next to Sophia. Sophia was waving her arm. *The last stunt! I forgot the last stunt.*

Abby ran across the mat.

"Where were you?" asked Emma.

"Lift her up now," directed Sophia.

"OK," said Abby. "Here we go."

Abby, Sophia and Kayla lifted Emma for the last stunt.

"Hold that pose," said Coach Tammy. She counted to eight. "OK, bring your flyers down."

The Glitter girls lowered Emma and Brianna to the mat.

"I'd like to practice that again," said Coach Tammy.

Me too, thought Abby.

Coach Tammy looked at her watch. "But it looks like we're out of time."

Abby saw the next group lined up on the mat. *Can't they wait just a few minutes,* thought Abby.

"Let's go line up," said Coach Tammy.

Abby looked at Emma. *But we're not ready!*

Out of Time

Abby took Emma's hand as they walked over to the line. Sophia was right behind them. "What happened to you two? You're going to make us lose!"

"No, we're not," said Abby. But Emma started crying

Sophia pointed at Emma. "She knows I'm right."

"Stop!" said Abby. "You're just making it worse."

"No, I'm not," said Sophia. "You did that all by yourself." Then she turned and walked away.

Emma cried even harder. Abby put her arm around her sister. "Don't listen to Sophia," said Abby. "You know how bossy she is."

"But," sobbed Emma. "But she's right."

"Well, yes," said Abby. She took a deep breath. "We did make mistakes. But that's because we were sick."

"It's not our fault," said Emma.

Taylor came over and put her arm around Emma too.

"No, it isn't," said Taylor. She looked at Abby. "It isn't your fault."

"But," said Abby, and she paused.

"But we're going on in a few minutes,"

said Taylor.

"We know how to do all the moves," said Abby. "Don't we, Emma?"

Emma stopped crying. "Yes, yes, we do."

"So what's the problem?" asked Taylor.

"They're in a different order now," said Abby.

"They switched them," said Emma, as she wiped away her tears. "It's not fair."

OK, thought Abby. *Now what do I say?* She looked at Taylor.

"Well," said Taylor. "We have to think of a way for you to remember."

"Like what?" said Abby.

"I'm thinking," said Taylor.

"I used to go up after the cheer," said Emma. "I could remember that."

"Well, now we go around in a circle after the cheer," said Abby.

"We cheer, then circle," said Taylor. "Cheer, circle. You can remember that, right?"

"Cheer, circle," repeated Abby. "That's easy." She knelt down next to Emma. "Can you remember?"

Emma nodded. "But what about the end?"

"Oh, I know that one," said Abby, and she smiled. "You always say that you're last."

"But I am!" said Emma.

"And what does Mom say to that?" asked Abby.

Emma shrugged her shoulders. "We saved the best for last."

"And that's what it will be," said Abby. "I'll be holding you up so everyone can see you."

"Oh," said Emma.

"Everyone looks at the flyer," said Abby.

"They do," said Taylor.

Emma thought for a minute. "I like this new ending better," she said. "Coach Tammy saved the best for last … me!"

Abby and Taylor laughed.

"That's right," said Abby. "Now let's go get in line. It's almost time to go on."

Now or Never

Here we go, thought Abby. She walked past the curtain and out onto the mat. The judges were sitting at tables facing the performers. And behind them was the audience.

Where's Mom? Abby looked up, trying to find her. Then she saw her. Mom was waving both of her hands in the air. Abby smiled. Then she walked to her place on the mat. Abby put her hand on her hip. Then she looked down. *Wait for it ...*

The music started.

"Presenting ... Big D Elite," said the deep voice.

Abby lifted her head. Emma and Brianna were in the first row. They did the back limber together. Then the next row, Liv and Kayla, did the back limber. *And here we go.* Abby, Taylor, Sophia and Maddie did the back limber together.

Then everyone went to their places for the first stunt. *Up you go, Emma!*

Abby, Sophia and Kayla held Emma high in the air. Then they walked with her to the middle of the mat. Emma reached out and touched Brianna's hand.

Nice, thought Abby.

The girls brought both the flyers down. Then they all did cartwheels. *Down, over and up.*

The four jumps were next. Abby jumped facing the judges. She lifted her arms to her side and touched them with her feet. *Toe touch!*

The Glitter girls all turned to the right and jumped again. Another turn and another jump. It was hard for everyone to jump at the same time, but they did it. Four times in a row!

Then it was time for the cartwheel circle. *This is our first circle*, thought Abby, as she did cartwheels out to the edge of the mat. Then she turned around. Abby waited for the other girls to finish their moves. Then it was time to go back to the middle for more stunts.

Abby did a thigh stand and held up

Emma. Emma lifted her back leg into the air. *Good.* Then Emma stepped down.

Sophia and Kayla came over. Abby helped Sophia and Kayla lift Emma. Then they carried her across the mat again. Emma touched Brianna's hand one more time.

Hold it and then let go. Abby held on tight as Emma did two more moves.

And down you go. Now for our cheer.

"Big D Elite, can't be beat.

We're the ones you want to meet!"

And now … Abby paused … *it's cheer, circle! Yes, I remember.*

Abby ran over to her spot for the second circle. *Yes, that's right.* She looked across the mat. Emma remembered too!

Here I go. One, two, three, four. Turn and step, arms out.

Five, six, seven, eight, arms up. And now *we do the last stunt.*

Abby ran over to lift up Emma. Sophia and Kayla helped her.

"We saved the best for last," said Abby.

"Me!" Emma smiled.

"Hurry up," commanded Sophia.

The three bases lifted Emma into the air.

Count to eight …

The music stopped, and the audience cheered. The girls lowered Emma to the mat.

"We did it!" said Abby.

"We'll see what the judges say," grumbled Sophia.

Abby watched as Sophia walked off the mat. *I did my best*, thought Abby. *That's what matters. I helped Emma, and we both did our best.*

Taylor ran over to Abby and Emma. "You remembered!"

"We saved the best for last," said Emma.

"Yes, we did," said Abby. She took

Emma's hand. Then Abby reached out her other hand to Taylor. Abby smiled as the three girls walked off the mat together, hand in hand. *The sleepover is tonight!*

BIG D ELITE
BIG D ELITE
BIG D ELITE

About the Author

Books have always been part of Anastasia Suen's life. Her mother started reading to her when she was a baby and took her to the library every week. She wrote her first picture book when she was eleven and has been writing ever since. She used to be an elementary school teacher, and now she visits classrooms to talk about being an author. She has published over 130 books, writes an Internet blog about children's books and teaches writing to college students. She's never been a cheerleader, but she can yell really loud!

Read them all!